Israel Mauduit

The Case of the Dissenting Ministers

Israel Mauduit

The Case of the Dissenting Ministers

ISBN/EAN: 9783337333898

Printed in Europe, USA, Canada, Australia, Japan

Cover: Foto ©Andreas Hilbeck / pixelio.de

More available books at **www.hansebooks.com**

THE

CASE

OF THE

DISSENTING MINISTERS.

ADDRESSED TO THE

LORDS SPIRITUAL AND TEMPORAL.

By ISRAEL MAUDUIT.

To which is added,
A COPY of the BILL propofed for
their Relief.

THE FOURTH EDITION.

LONDON:

Printed for J. WILKIE, at No. 71, in St. Paul's
Church-Yard. MDCCLXXII.

THE following Cafe has been written and printed, without the Knowledge of any One of the Diffenting Minifters, concerned in the prefent Application to Parliament: The Author defires therefore, if any Thing contained in it fhould be judged improper, that the Blame may fall upon himfelf only, and not be imputed to the Prejudice of a Caufe, which he wifhes to ferve; and which he thinks deferving the Patronage of every Friend to Civil and Religious Liberty.

THE

CASE

OF THE

DISSENTING MINISTERS, &c.

THE Reafonablenefs of Toleration, has been fo demonftrably proved by Mr. *Locke*, that no Man, fince the Publication of his Letters, has ventured to difpute it.

THE Benefits of Toleration, this Nation, for more than fourfcore Years, has been experiencing.

AT the Revolution, that great Æra of Liberty and of Proteftantifm, one of the firft Concerns of Parliament was to grant to all Proteftants diffenting from the Church of *England*, a Liberty of meet-

B

ing together for the Exercise of their own religious Worship.

In the Year 1689, when the Toleration Act was paffed, the Diffenters were ftricter Calvinifts, and more zealous Adherents to the Doctrinal Parts of the Thirty-nine Articles, than many of the Eftablifhed Clergy themfelves were.

The Act of Toleration therefore, by excufing them from the Articles of Difcipline, granted them Relief in all which they wanted; and, by directing that they fhould fubfcribe the reft, required no more of them than what they then believed.

From the Writings of Bifhop *Taylor*, *Stillingfleet*, *Tillotfon*, *Burnet*, *Hoadly*, *Clarke*, and the beft Church of *England* Divines; from a more exact Study of the Holy Scriptures; and from the general Improvement in all Parts of Knowledge, which is naturally made in a Courfe of Years, many of the Diffenters now find their Opinions altered in fome

of

of thefe Articles, which had not then
been fo carefully examined, and cannot
fubfcribe.

THEY do not take upon themfelves to
judge of others : But, after diligently
endeavouring to underftand the Mean-
ing of them, and ferioufly examining
their own Hearts, they find that they
cannot declare their folemn Affent and
Confent to them, confiftently with Sin-
cerity and a good Confcience.

HENCE it arifes, that the Intention of
the Toleration Act is fruftrated : And,
though at the Time of paffing, it meant
to give the Diffenters a legal Right to
the Exercife of divine Worfhip in their
own Manner, and at that Time actually
did give it them ; yet now it does not.
The Act is rendered ineffectual, and their
Minifters ftand expofed to the Penal
Laws of *Charles* II. by the Toleration's
being made to depend upon a Condition,
which at that Time they could with Sin-
cerity comply with, but which now they
cannot.

B 2   IN

In these their Scruples, whether they are right or wrong is not the Question; but whether they are *criminally* wrong: Crimes only being the Object of Punishment.

No Man in this enlightened Age will say, that a Diffenting Minifter's merely Preaching to his People is a Crime, which merits Fining, Imprifoning, and Banifhment; or that his adminiftring the Sacrament merits an additional Fine of one Hundred Pounds; five and twenty of which are given as an Encouragement to the Informer.

No Man would wifh to fee thefe Severities put into Execution.

Is it not then a Difgrace to our Statute-Book, to fuffer Laws to ftand there, which ought never to be executed?

In the two Reigns preceding the Revolution, the penal Laws were the chief

Inftruments

Inftruments in the Hands of a popifh King and popifh Minifters, to divide Proteftants, and make them hate one another worfe than Papifts: and the Severities of them were made Ufe of on Purpofe to force the Diffenters to petition for a general Toleration; and to prepare the Nation to receive fuch a one, as fhould include both Papifts and Diffenters.

Is it not then the moft natural Method of expreffing our Regard to *Proteftant Chriftianity*, to abolifh thofe fevere Laws, which were made Ufe of by Papifts on Purpofe to deftroy it?

MIGHT we not appeal to the fpiritual Part of our Legiflators, whether it be agreeable to the Precept of our great ' Mafter, to bind thefe grievous Burdens, and to retain thefe Terrors over others, which cannot poffibly be of any Benefit to the eftablifhed Church, and which all Men would fo heavily feel when laid upon themfelves?

Is it confiftent with the Spirit of Law-making, or did any wife Legiflature ever alledge as an Argument for the continuing of a Law, that it is fo very unreafonable that there is no Danger of any one's putting it in Execution?

SHALL *then*, it may be afked, *profligate and vicious Men be allowed to preach, and corrupt the Manners of the People?*

VICIOUS and profligate Men doubtlefs ought, if poffible, to be kept out of every Church, but Subfcriptions will keep them out of none. What Hold can be had from Principle on Men, who are void of Principle? Or what Security in the Truth of Men, who deny or defpife the facred Obligations of it? Make as many Articles as you will, *they* will fubfcribe them all.

SHALL *then Deifts or profane Scoffers be fuffered to preach? and from the Pulpit undermine the Chriftian Religion?*
deny

deny the Trinity? or revile the Service of our Liturgy?

A DEIST *upon Principle* would never wifh to be a Preacher of the Gofpel; and he that has no Principle will certainly go into the Church, where there is the moft to be got by it.

As to the Doctrine of the Trinity, that is fufficiently guarded by the 10th of King *William:* An Act, which needs no additional Severities to protect a Doctrine, concerning which good Men in all Ages have been of different Opinions, and which many great Divines of the Church of *England* have not thought to be of fo much Importance. They, however, who think it of the moft Importance, will find themfelves by that Act armed with all the neceffary Powers for its Maintenance. Nor will any one, who reads the Act, find himfelf in the leaft Degree more difpofed to impeach that Doctrine after the paffing of this Bill, than he was before.

" AS

" An Incapacity for any Office eccle-
" fiaftic, civil, or military, in the firft
" Inftance, and an Inability to plead any
" Action at Law, to be a Guardian, or
" Executor, or Legatee, and the fuffer-
" ing Imprifonment for three Years, in
" the fecond Inftance," are Terrors
which are abundantly fufficient for the
Purpofe, but which nothing fhort of
Infallibility can juftify.

As to the Liturgy, that is abundantly
fecured by the 1ft of *Elizabeth*, which
ordains, that " If any Perfon fhall in
" Plays, Songs, or Rimes, or *by other*
" *open Words* declare or fpeak any thing
" in the derogation, depraving, or de-
" fpifing of the fame Book, (of Common
" Prayer) or of any thing therein con-
" tained, or any Part thereof, he fhall
" for the firft Offence, forfeit a Hun-
" dred Marks, or fuffer Six Months
" Imprifonment; for the fecond, Four
" hundred Marks, or fuffer Twelve
" Months Imprifonment; and for the
" third, fhall forfeit all his Goods and
" Chattels,

" Chattels, and fhall fuffer Imprifonment
" for Life."

BUT *fhall Enthufiafts of all Sorts be
fuffered to get into Pulpits? Men who
defpife the written Word of God, and pretend to peculiar Infpiration ?*

IF any fuch *fhould* arife, in vain will
human Laws oppofe their Authority
againft Men, who think that they act
under the divine : And human Prudence
will judge it much wifer to fuffer wild
Enthufiafm to vent itfelf in its own Way,
and evaporate fo much the fooner.

BUT, in Fact, who are the reputed
Enthufiafts of the prefent Times? the
Enthufiafts, againft whom many of our
Bifhops have fo earneftly engaged ? Are
we not directed to feek for them among
the Methodifts? Men, that are fprung
out of the *Church,* and not from the
Diffenters; and Men, who, of all others,
are the greateft Zealots for the thirty-
nine Articles ?

SHOULD

SHOULD any diftempered Imagina-
tion, or monaftic Gloom, ftill raife up
to itfelf Spectres of I know not what
Herefies and Schifms, and fancy that
unknown and untried Evils are to arife
out of this Exemption; even fuch ima-
ginary Terrors may well fubfide, when
it is confidered, that the Diffenters preaching without fubfcribing is not a new
Experiment to be made now; but is a
Practice, which has already fubfifted for
thefe forty or fifty Years paft, and no
evil Confequences have arifen from it:
And furely their making the folemn
Declaration, which is now propofed, is
at leaft a better Security, than their
making none at all.

WHATEVER Strefs the prefent Right
Reverend Bench may lay on enforcing
Subfcription upon Diffenters, their learned Predeceffors in King *William's* Time
did not judge it a Matter of quite fo
much Importance: for the Toleration Bill,
as framed by the Bifhops and Judges in
the Houfe of Lords, and fent down to
the other, did not enjoin it: and the
Obliga-

Obligation to *subscribe*, was inserted by the Commons.

By the present Toleration Act, the Quakers are not required to subscribe any one of the Articles of the Church of *England*. The Makers of that Act, therefore, could not have thought it criminal to doubt of any of the thirty-four doctrinal Articles, nor have thought it necessary to prevent from preaching Men, who did not subscribe them. Even that single Declaration, which the Quakers do make, had never been thought of by the Legislature, if they themselves had not voluntarily offered it. *Quod imprudens Factum,* says Mr. *Locke* [*], *multi inter illos, & Cordatiores, valde dolent.* If the Church was not injured, nor the Consciences of Churchmen violated, by the allowing of one Set of Dissenters to preach, without any Obligation to subscribe the Articles; how then can either of these be affected, by

C 2 allow-

---

allowing the fame Exemption to the others?

THE Toleration in *Scotland* requires no Subfcription to the Articles of the eftablifhed Church of *Scotland*.

BUT what is decifive upon this Point is, that the Toleration in *Ireland* requires no Subfcription.

IF the Church has been fafe in *Ireland*, ever fince the 6th of *George* I. though the Diffenters there do not fubfcribe the Articles, may not the Church be juft as fafe in *England* as it is in *Ireland*?

IN fhort, Men may fearch for what diftant Pretences they pleafe; but the common Senfe of Mankind will ever be againft the Law as it now ftands. Is there any Man fuch a Stranger to the Right of private Judgment, as to fay, that the not being able to give a folemn Affent and Confent to all and every one of the doctrinal Articles, is a Crime merit-

meriting a pofitive Punifhment from the State ? Is there any Man fuch a Stranger to the firft Principles of Toleration, as to fay, that a diffenting Minifter's preaching a Sermon in his own licenfed Place of Worfhip is a Crime deferving the pofitive Punifhment of the Magiftrate ? If then neither of thefe Things are Crimes in themfelves, can two innocent Actions put together make a criminal one ? Yes : perhaps it may be replied, as the Law now ftands, he fhould not preach without having fubfcribed. True, it does fay fo, and that is the very Evil we complain of : that the Law, not intentionally, but accidentally, makes an innocent Action criminal, and punifhes it more feverely than Actions, which are really criminal : which is the very Evil, which the Toleration Act meant intentionally to redrefs, and which we now afk to have actually redreffed.

But *the Diffenters*, we have been told, *are not the fame now, that they were formerly* ;

formerly; *for they have changed their Opinions*. The Diffenters are not changed from their Predeceffors, more than
the Clergy of the Church of *England*
are changed from theirs. But in Fact,
both of them, by ftudying the Scriptures
more carefully, have found Reafon to
alter their Opinions as to many doctrinal
Articles. The Clergy of the Church of
England changed firft, and many of the
Diffenters have fince. See the Account
which the learned Bifhop of *Winchefter*
gives of this Matter; who certainly was
well acquainted with the State of the Englifh Clergy*. " The Queftion now before
" us may foon be refolved, by afking,
" Which is the beft and fecureft Way of
" knowing exactly, what the Doctrine
" of any particular Church, fuppofe the
" Church of *England*, delivered at the
" Time of the Reformation. Whether
" by confulting the Writings of particu-
" lar Divines many Years after that
" Period, or from authentic Acts and
" Decla-

---

* Hoadly's Sermon on contending for the Faith.

" Declarations made and recorded at the
" very Time?——For this Inftance is
" very proper to clear up what I have
" been faying; as it will prove to us,
" beyond all Contradiction, that the Doc-
" trine, even of a particular Church; and
" a Doctine recorded and fet down in as
" accurate a Manner, as was thought
" neceffary *for the avoiding Diverfity of*
" *Opinions*; that even fuch a Doctrine
" may, in fifty Years Time, come to un-
" dergo fome Alterations; and in a few
" Years more, to be entirely changed, in
" the Writings and Difcourfes of moft of
" the Members of the fame Church. I
" mean particularly the Points of Doc-
" trine, called the Five Points, relating
" to Juftification, and God's Decrees,
" and the like: Which were at firft
" efteemed as Fundamental, and even
" Effential to the Church of *Chrift*, as
" any others can be; and yet have been
" at length much changed by gradual
" Alterations." Have the Diffenters
made any greater Change in their Opinions, than what this wife Bifhop tells
us has been made by the Clergy? or do
                                    either

either of us merit Fine and Imprifonment for our underſtanding the holy Scripture better than our Forefathers ? If under
the preſent State of the Law the pious
Biſhop of *Wincheſter* did not think proper
to reprehend his Clergy for ſubſcribing
the ſame Articles, though he knew that
their Faith was *changed*; ſurely his Suc-
ceſſors will not hold us puniſhable, who
do not ſubſcribe the Articles, becauſe our
Faith is not the *ſame* ?

But it has been ſaid, *If we grant the
Diſſenters this, they may aſk for ſomething
more*.*

If this Meaſure be wrong, there muſt
be ſome good Reaſon to be urged againſt
it : but if inſtead of aſſigning any, we
only allege, that it may lead to ſomething elſe which is wrong; is not that
Allegation a tacit Acknowledgment, that
this Requeſt, at leaſt, is not unreaſonable ? And is not the granting that
which is reaſonable, the beſt Preparative
for,

---

* The Repeal of the Teſt-Act.

for, and the moſt ſolid Juſtification of our refuſing that which is unreaſonable?

CAN it be expected that other Men will give themſelves the Trouble of preciſely marking out the Diſtinction between reaſonable and unreaſonable Requeſts; when thoſe, who are the beſt able, decline it, and chooſe to give an indiſcriminate Refuſal to them both?

NOT to add, that the exempting of their Preachers from Penalties, and the entitling of their Laity to Honours, are very different Things.

IS *then this Application particularly neceſſary at this Time? Or do any incline to put the Laws in Force againſt them?*

No, they do not. But that is the very Reaſon which makes this the proper Time for them to apply for Relief. Such is the unhappy Situation of the Diſſenters, that, as the Law now ſtands, Men always have it in their *Power* to perſecute them: they have an entire Confidence in the Lenity and Wifdom of Government, that they have not the *Will* to do it; and it is this favourable Difpofition, which makes the prefent the only proper Seafon to afk to be fecured againft future Danger. Should there arife another Race of civil or ecclefiaftical Governors, who fhould have the *Will* to perfecute them, it would be to little Purpofe for the Diffenters to afk of *them* to give up the *Power* to do it. They believe that every Lord of Parliament is convinced of the Equity and of the Benefit of Toleration : They thankfully acknowledge the Felicity of the Age, and are fatisfied that no Part of the Legiflature would defire to fee thefe fevere Laws put in Force againft them : They are fure that no Lord of Parliament is fo far divefted of Humanity, as to become *himfelf* their Perfecutor : They believe that none would wifh to fee any one elfe perfecute them; and it is that very Perfuafion which makes them now apply to the Equity of the Houfe, and beg that their Lordfhips would not leave it

in

in the *Power* of any one elfe to perfecute
them. 'Tis from Friends only they can
afk for Security; they well know that
they muft not hope for it from their
Enemies.

THERE may be Bigots ftill left in the
Kingdom, who may fecretly wifh for an
Opportunity to put thefe Penalties in
Force: But even fuch Men know that
the Principles of Perfecution in this enlightened Age, are fo extremely odious,
that they dare not openly avow them.
Such Men, therefore, at prefent, will
only fay, " *What need* of altering the
Law, fince we don't intend to make
Ufe of it?" This was the Language of
narrow Minds at the Time of paffing the
Toleration Act. *Some propofed*, fays
Bifhop *Burnet* *, *that the Act fhould be
only temporary ; as a neceffary Reftraint
upon the Diffenters: That they might de-
mean themfelves fo as to merit the Continuance of it, when the Term of Years now*

offered

---

* Hift. Vol. ii, p. 10.

offered might be expired. **But this was**
rejected: There was now an universal In-
clination to pass the Act; whereas there
might not be the same good Disposition
at another Time. That House of Lords
was too wise and generous to adopt
any of the Pretences for Persecution.
We have lived to see the Wisdom of it:
And must have experienced the Benefits
of Toleration for so many Years since
to very little Purpose, if in this more
enlightened Age *our* Sentiments are not
as liberal as *theirs,* and if the *present*
House of Lords is not at least as generous
as *that* was.

THIS Plea of Non-Intention to exe-
cute them, is not a new Argument, but
has been the Pretence for the continuing
of all penal Laws. It does not indeed
give us the most favourable Opinion of
this Argument to consider, that it ope-
rates in just the contrary Way to all other
Reasonings. The *direct* Rule of civil
Politicks is: the more absurd the Law,
the more Reason for repealing it. But
the

the Rule of ecclefiaftic Politics runs *inverfly*; the more abfurd the Law, the lefs Reafon for repealing it. The moft cruel and abfurd of all penal Laws, was the Writ *de Hæretico comburendo*. The *Marian* Perfecution and Bifhop *Bonner*'s Fires had put it out of Countenance, and the Argument of Non-Intention in that Cafe was ftrongeft of all. It is not neceffary to fay how it was ufed in the Year 1677, when that Writ was taken away. In the prefent Application, which is only for taking away the Writ *de Hæretico imprifonando*, this Argument is not quite fo ftrong. The Diffenters for their own Sakes don't wifh to weaken it.

BUT the Statute which came the neareft to that for Burning them, was the 35th of *Elizabeth:* by which the Puritans were condemned to abjure the Realm; and, if they returned, to fuffer Death. In the Year 1681, when the Eyes of the Nation were open'd, and it was feen that the Defign of the

Court

Court was to bring in Popery, under the Cover of executing the penal Laws againſt the Diſſenters, a Motion was made in the Houſe of Commons for the Repeal of this very ſevere Act. The Bill paſt eaſily there : But, ſays Biſhop *Burnet*, " It went heavily in the Houſe of
" Lords; for many of the Biſhops, tho'
" they were not for putting that Law in
" Execution, which had never been
" done, but in one ſingle Inſtance ; yet
" they thought the Terror of it was of
" ſome Uſe; and that the repealing it
" might make the Party more inſolent.
" On the Day of the Prorogation, the
" Bill ought to have been offered to
" the King; but the Clerk of the
" Crown, by the King's particular
" Order, withdrew the Bill. The King
" had no Mind openly to deny it ; but
" he had leſs Mind to paſs it."

IN the Morning, before they were prorogued, " two Votes were carried
" in the Houſe of a very extraordinary
" Nature : the one was, that the Laws
" made

" made againſt Recuſants ought not to
" be executed againſt any but thoſe of
" the Church of *Rome*. That was in-
" deed the primary Intention of the
" Law : yet all Perſons who came not
" to Church, and did not receive the
" Sacrament once a Year, were within
" the Letter of the Law. The other
" Vote was, that it was the Opinion
" of that Houſe, that the Laws againſt
" Diſſenters ought not to be executed *."
Yet how much ſoever the Nation was
then alarmed with the Danger of Popery,
and how averſe ſoever to Severities againſt
Diſſenters, no ſooner had the King diſ-
ſolved his *Oxford* Parliament, but Addreſ-
ſes came up to Court from all Parts of the
Kingdom ; " ſome of which reflected
" ſeverely on the Non-Conformiſts; and
" thanked the King for his not repealing
" that Act of the 35th of *Elizabeth*, which
" they prayed might be put in Execu-
" tion †." Whatever generous Sentiments

for

---

for Liberty of Confcience may at prefent
prevail, have not the Diffenters juft Reafon to be apprehenfive, that the Tide of
popular Opinion may not run always the
fame Way ?

BUT *why could not they have kept their*
own Council, and not have difcovered this
their weak Side to the World?

THEY *have* kept their own Council
for fifty Years together, and few Secrets
relating to large Bodies of Men have
been kept longer.

THEY were now called to this Application by the Voice of the Publick, and
muft have been ftrangely wanting to their
own Safety to have neglected it.

WITHOUT their *Knowledge*, but not
without their *Thanks*, their Cafe was
publifhed *, and brought under the immediate

---

* By the learned and very ingenious Dean of
Gloucefter.

mediate View of the Legiflature. In
the Houfe of Commons many Gentlemen on both Sides of the Queftion then
before them, voluntarily declared their
Senfe of the Hardfhip laid upon the
Diffenters, in being obliged to fubfcribe the Articles of the Church, to
which they did not belong, and in
which they did not feek Promotion : and
fignified their Readinefs to confent to a
Bill for their Relief. Could they refufe
to liften to fuch an Invitation ?

THE Event has proved that they
judged rightly of the Occafion, that that
was the real Senfe of the Houfe, and
that *one* Part at leaft of Government was
not againft them : but nine Members
having on any Day been to be found
to vote againft this Bill.

Now therefore fince this publick
Notice, their Toleration ftands upon ten-
derer Ground than it did before : Their
Danger is increafed by its Notoriety, and
they are put under the Neceffity of flying
to the Juftice of Parliament for Safety.

E THEY

THEY are now compelled to fay aloud, what before they always faid to *themfelves*: that, as innocent Subjects, they have a Right to owe their Security to the Protection of the *Laws* of their Country, and not merely to the Favour of its *Governors*.

AND though they thankfully acknowledge, that hitherto they have been fheltered from Profecutions by the Favour of Government, yet, that is a Screen, which is now feen through, and may not hereafter prove fufficient for their Protection.

SHOULD evil minded Perfons take up the Trade of informing againft them, what is it, which can be expected?

MEN may wifh, as much as they pleafe, that the Diffenters would fubfcribe the Articles; and they may condemn their Minifters, as much as they pleafe, for not fubfcribing; but is there any Lord, Temporal or Spiritual, who will fay, that

that he wishes to revive the Severities of the *Bartholomew-day*, 1662 ; when two thousand dissenting Ministers were turned out of their Livings ? If no one will avow this, what good End then can be answered, by letting loose Informers upon them, and running the Risk of creating Uneasiness in every County in the Kingdom? merely for the sake of forcing the Articles of the Church upon Men, who do not belong to the Church, and who therefore have nothing to do with them ?

They who are less affected by religious Considerations, may perhaps be more disposed to attend to the Subject, when considered in a political Light. Whatever we may think of the present Times, there may come a Prince, and a Set of Ministers, Laymen or Ecclesiastics, who may form a Design to enslave us. Should such an evil Day come, is there any one Thing, which they would more desire, or which would be a greater Furtherance in the Execution of their

E 2   Design,

Defign, than their having large Bodies of Men all over the Kingdom, obnoxious to penal Laws, and fubject to their Mercy? Would any good *Englifhman* then wifh to leave it in the Power of fome future bad Minifter, to be able to intimate to the diffenting Teacher in any Borough in the Kingdom, Sir, give your Vote for my Candidate, and ufe your Intereft for him with your People in the Corporation Town where you preach, or expect to be banifhed out of it, and to be fent to the County Jail, if ever you come within five Miles of it.

BUT *this*, it has been faid, *is a new Attack upon the Church, added to feveral others made in the fame* Seffion.

THE taking innocent Men out of the Reach of Informers, and delivering them from a Liablenefs to Fines and Imprifonment, an Attack upon the Church?

DOES the Church then live by the Power of perfecuting other Men, that

do

do not belong to it? or can the rendering innocent Men unhappy tend to its Edification?

Do Men wish to retain the Power of perfecuting as a *Support* to the Church? or as an *Ornament* to the Church? They cannot furely pay it a worfe Compliment than to fuppofe either.

Is our holy Religion the fafer, or are Churchmen the happier for their having a Power of harraffing Diffenters? Far be it from me to fuppofe, that the Members of any Chriftian Church fhould wifh to indulge fo unchriftian a Pleafure, as that of holding other Men at their Mercy. But if there fhould be any fuch unhappy Difpofition, it is furely fit that innocent Men fhould be put out of the Reach of it.

But *we cannot in Confcience affent to this*, has been the Language of fome.

The Judgment of Confcience doubtlefs is facred, and every Man is bound

to

to obey it: but if Confcience will not permit our Legiflators to allow the free Liberty of preaching to Men, who make the folemn Declaration in this Bill, will not Confcience much more oblige them not to leave this Liberty of preaching to Men, who make no Declaration at all? So far therefore as Confcience is concerned in retaining the Obligation to fubfcribe, Confcience muft be concerned in enforcing it: and if the Plea of Confcience be brought for keeping up this Sword of Juftice ftill hanging over their Heads, furely the Diffenters have juft Caufe to tremble, left the fame Plea of Confcience may be hereafter urged for the letting it fall on them. The beft Argument, which the Oppofers of this Bill have hitherto offered for the Continuance of the Law in its prefent State, is, that they never intend to make Ufe of it: but the Plea of Confcience fupercedes all thefe merciful Difpofitions. And when the retaining of this Law is confidered as the Caufe of God, which it muft be to make it a Matter of

Con-

Confcience, the exerting it may but too eafily come to be thought doing him good Service. Charity itfelf therefore muft dictate to every lay Lord the Amendment of the prefent Law, in order to preferve the Confciences of Churchmen from being entangled in the Execution of it.

BUT, we have been told, *a Heathen, a Deift, or even a Mahometan, might fubfcribe the Declaration in this Bill.* The Declaration propofed is in the following Form: *I A. B. declare, as in the Prefence of Almighty God, that I believe that the holy Scriptures of the Old and New Teftament contain a Revelation of the Mind and Will of God, and that I receive them as the Rule of my Faith and Practice.* Whatever may be the Language of Ignorance, the Diffenters hope that their Chriftianity will not be queftioned by thofe, who fhould better underftand the folemn Nature of this Declaration, and the exprefs determinate Import of thefe Words. If it fhould be, all which

they

they have to reply is, they hope that they shall ever tremble at the Thought of committing so gross an Act of Insincerity and Impiety. Will a Mahometan renounce his Coran, and say that he receives the New Testament *for the Rule of his Faith and Practice ?*

If they had been capable of such Prevarication in the Sight of Almighty God, they needed not to have come to Parliament to be relieved from Subscription.

But in as much as such uncharitable Suppositions have been made, they beg Leave now to add, as the uniform and avowed Principle of the Dissenters, that, as they believe the holy Scriptures to be the Word of God, so they receive them with that supreme Reverence, which is due to them *as* the Word of God, and which is due to no other Writing *but* the Word of God. That they hold it their Duty to believe all which they find in the Word of God, and that no Man is bound to believe,

and

and much lefs has any Right to compel
them to profefs they believe any Thing,
which they do not find to be contained
in the Word of God. That they willingly read any human Compofition pro-
feffing to help them to the Underftanding
of the Word of God; but that they
receive no human Compofition as an
authoritative Interpretation of Scripture;
becaufe that is an exalting of that human
Compofition *above* the Word of God:
it is the making the Compofition of
Man the Teft of the Word of God,
whereas they have ever learned to make
the Word of God the Teft of every human Compofition. They believe that
the holy Scriptures are the only and the
fufficient Rule of Faith and Practice,
and can fubmit to the Authority of no
human Decifions as a fupplemental
Amendment to them. They believe the
holy Scriptures to contain the Whole of
that Revelation, which God has been
pleafed to make to us, and dare not
acknowledge any fuch Defects in that
Revelation, as to need the Affiftance of
human Wifdom to fupply them. They

F   fee

fee that all the *Works* of God are perfect in their feveral Kinds, and they believe that God never gave his *Word* for Man to mend.

THESE have been the unvaried Senti-ments of the Diffenters, and they are confirmed in them by the concurrent Senfe of the greateft Writers of the Church of *England*, from the Refor-mation to this Day. At the Time, when the *Englifh* Government, and other proteftant States, feparated themfelves from the Church of *Rome*, the authori-tative Interpretations of Scripture, and the Decifions of the Church, were all againft them. *They* were then the Schif-matics and the Heretics. The firft Re-formers therefore all appealed from thefe Decifions to the Scriptures themfelves, and acknowledged *them* as the only Rule of Faith. " By the Religion of Pro-
" teftants, (fays the great *Chillingworth)*
" I do not underftand the Doctrine of
" *Luther*, of *Calvin*, or *Melancton*, or
" the Confeffion of *Augufta* or *Geneva*,
" nor the Catechifin of *Heidelberg*, nor
" the

" the Articles of the Church of *England*;
" but that, wherein they all agree, and
" which they all fubfcribe, as a perfect
" Rule of their Faith and Actions, that
" is the *Bible*, the *Bible*, the *Bible*, I
" fay, the *Bible* only is the Religion of
" Proteftants—In a Word, there is no
" fufficient Certainty, but of Scripture
" only, for any confidering Man to
" build upon. This therefore, and this
" only, I have Reafon to believe: this
" I will profefs: according to this I
" will live, and for this, if there be
" Occafion, I will not only willingly,
" but even gladly lofe my Life; though
" I fhould be forry that Chriftians fhould
" take it from me. Propofe me any
" Thing out of this Book, and require
" whether I believe or no, and, feem
" it never fo incomprehenfible to human
" Reafon, I will fubfcribe it with Hand
" and Heart, as knowing, no Demon-
" ftration can be ftronger than this:
" God hath faid fo, therefore it is true.
" In other Things, I will take no Man's
" Liberty of Judgment from him, nei-
" ther fhall any Man take mine from

F 2   " me.

" me.' I will think no Man the worfe
" Man, nor the' worfe Chriftian : I will
" love no Man the lefs for differing in
" Opinion from me; and what Mea-
" fure I mete to others, I expect from
" them again.   I am fully affured, that
" God does not, and therefore that Men
" ought not, to require any more of
" any Man than this, to believe the
" Scriptures to be God's Word, to en-
" deavour to find the true Senfe of it,
" and to live according to it."

THE pious and very learned Bifhop of
Winchefter's Sermon on contending for
the Faith is wholly employed upon this
Argument.

" THERE are fome Chriftians, (fays
" he) and a very numerous Body of
" Men they are, who know no other
" Guide but the living Guide of the
" prefent Church, and acknowledge no
" other Faith for *the Faith once delivered*
" *to the Saints* about feventeen hundred
" Years ago, but that which is now de-
" livered to them by their prefent Rulers
" as

" as fuch. The greater Part of thefe
" take a very fhort Method of eftablifh-
" ing this Point, and that is, by laying
" down the Infallibility of the prefent
" Church.

" But this is a Point fo grofs, and fo
" utterly void of all Proof, that a great
" Body of the Chriftian World have
" broke loofe from the Power of this
" Monfter. And, in Order to this, they
" had no other Way, but to declare for
" the New Teftament itfelf, as the only
" Guide, or Rule of Faith; the only
" Deliverer of this Faith to us of later
" Ages. And this is the very Rule, I
" have now laid down. But when this
" comes to be put in Practice; too many
" of the fame Perfons, who have fet it
" up as the only Guide, turn round on
" a fudden, and let us know that they
" mean by it, not thofe facred original
" Writings themfelves, but the Inter-
" pretations, or Senfe put upon them
" by our fpiritual Superiors: To which
" we are fometimes faid to be obliged,
" and bound in Duty to fubmit; and
" fome-

" fometimes are allowed a Liberty of
" Examination : But in effect, put under
" an Obligation to find that to be Truth,
" which is taught by thefe Leaders.

" But ought we not to pay a Regard
" to thofe whofe Bufinefs it is to find out
" the Truth, and to difpenfe it to us ?
" Yes undoubtedly : The Regard of feri-
" ous Attention, and the Refpect of a due
" Examination ; but not the Submiffion
" due only to Infallibility. Shall we
" not fubmit our low Underftandings to
" the higher Underftandings of others ?
" Or fhall we pretend to oppofe our
" Judgements to thofe of our Superiors ?
" Let thefe, and the like Queftions be
" afked concerning the chriftian Laity in
" all the popifh Countries ; and thofe
" of our Church will unanimoufly an-
" fwer, No : The Rule is quite other-
" wife. Nay with regard to the Refor-
" mation, it has been long ago with one
" Confent faid, that it was a glorious
" Thing not to fubmit to the Voice of
" any Men, but to referve that Regard for
" God and for Chrift in matters of Faith.
" I can-

" I CANNOT but obferve, that, in order
" to preferve this Faith, delivered in thofe
" antient Books, entire ; the moft fecure,
" as well as the moft chriftian Way, is
" to preferve the old Words, and the old
" Language, of thofe Books, as unvaried
" and unchanged as poffible.   The Rea-
" fon is plain, becaufe they are the
" Words, in which it pleafed *God* it
" fhould at firft be delivered. And there-
" fore, though many Perfons may mif-
" take in their different Apprehenfions
" concerning the Senfe of thefe Words;
" yet we may be fure, whilft we retain
" thefe Words, that we retain what *God*
" himfelf has feen fit fhould be delivered
" and tranfmitted to us, as the beft Con-
" veyance, all Things confidered, of the
" Faith required of us.

" I AM fenfible it is faid, *that Herefies*
" *arofe*, i. e. that fome Men differed
" from others, in their Notions founded
" upon thefe Words: And therefore, it
" was thought neceffary to change the
" Language, in which this Faith was
" delivered to us. But did not *Almighty*
                                        " *God*

" *God* forefee this great Evil of Difference
" of Opinion, in the Points in which
" Men have fince differed ? He did :
" And yet he left our Faith delivered in
" thofe Words, which are faid to have
" been the Foundation of thofe Diffe-
" rences. Or, are we wifer than *God*, in
" chufing more effectual Words to this
" Purpofe, than thofe in which the
" Perfons commiffioned by him delivered
" his Will? Who will fay this ? Or did
" he appoint, that in After-ages the
" antient Language fhould be totally
" changed, for a new Syftem of Words ;
" and that the Faith of Chriftians fhould
" be delivered over again in Novel Ex-
" preffions ? If he did, let a plain Text
" be produced ; and not fuch a confe-
" quential Argument, of the Ufefulnefs
" or Fitnefs of it, as may be urged,
" even for the Popifh Infallibility itfelf.

" B u t when new Language has,
" by the help of fuch an Argument,
" been introduced ; what has been the
" Effect ? Good and honeft Men *alone*
" have

" have been the Sufferers. These have
" been cramped and difturbed, and, per-
" haps, deprived of all worldly Privi-
" leges by it. The difhoneft, and un-
" thinking, and flavifh Minds have
" always rejoiced in fuch an earthly
" Peculium, as this Method fecures to
" them. And, if we confult Experience,
" the new Words invented for the Secu-
" rity of the Faith, with regard both to
" learned and unlearned, have been gene-
" rally fuch as have increafed, and not
" diminifhed Herefies and Schifms : hard
" Terms, metaphyfical and abftrufe
" Expreffions, ambiguous themfelves,
" though introduced under pretence of
" avoiding Ambiguity ; utterly unintel-
" ligible to the Unlearned, who yet are
" to be faved by Faith as well as others ;
" and eternally debated amongft the
" Learned. And thus it will always
" be, when Men become wifer in their
" own Conceit to prevent Evils, than
" *God* himfelf."

THESE are the Sentiments of one of
the greateft Writers of the Church of Eng-

land :

land : And we believe that **no greater** Writer of his Order will arise to contradict them. One of the greatest of them, to his Honour, has, in his *Writings* at least, declared for as liberal a Toleration, as Bishop *Hoadly* himself has.

UNDER these Authorities may not the Diffenters make their Appeal to Heathens, Deifts, and Mahometans, to whom they have on this Occafion been fo very injurioufly compared, and afk even of *them* to judge, Whether, as Chriftians, they can in any better Manner prove their Reverence to *Chrift*, their great Mafter and Lawgiver, than by acknowledging no other Authority but his? Or better exprefs their Belief of his Gofpel, than *by receiving it as the Revelation of the Mind and Will of God, and as the Rule of their Faith and Practice*, and by admitting of no human Additions to be made to it?

BUT whatever may be the Practice of others, upon which they do not prefume to judge,

judge, thefe are the Principles, to which, as Chriftians and as Proteftants, they think themfelves bound to adhere. And they humbly hope that none of the Servants of *Chrift*, their common Lord and Mafter, whofe Coming to publifh his Gofpel was announced by the Declaration of Peace and Good Will to Mankind, and at whofe fecond Coming we muft all account for the Ufes we have made of it ; they hope that no Proteftant Profeffor of the Gofpel of Peace will think, that that Gofpel can be a Warrant for their obliging other Chriftians, not belonging to their Church, to violate their Confciences by fubfcribing to human Articles of Faith, which they do not fee to be contained in the Word of *God*, or for their holding them fubject to Fines and Imprifonments, if they do not.

BUT what are the Diffenters ? and what have been their Doings, that they fhould fo often hear themfelves treated as Deifts, or as Enthufiafts ? Their Predeceffors of the laft Century all fubfcribed

the

the Articles, and are therefore beyond Exception. And as to thofe of the pre-fent, let the Writings of the late Lord Barrington and of Sir Richard Ellis; let the Commentaries of a Pierce, a Benfon, a Doddrige, a Lowman, and a Taylor, upon the different Parts of the New Tef-tament; let the numerous Sermons print-ed by others; let the learned labours of a Jones or a Lardner, the manly Devo-tions of a Grove or a Watts, the com-prehenfive Views of a Prieftley, the judi-cious Writings of a Farmer or a Bourn, the Works of an Amory, a Price, or a Furneaux, with other Members even of the prefent Committee; let thefe all teftify, whether the Diffenters are not ca-pable of fpeaking the Words of *Truth and Sobernefs* as well as other Men.

AND upon what Ground are they to be charged with Deifm? The Number of Diffenting Minifters may not perhaps amount to more than a Tenth Part of the Clergy of the Church of *England.* Nor have we at our private Academies the

the Advantage of fuch Libraries, as are to
be found at the two public Univerfities :
Yet, as often as our common Faith has
been attacked; the Diffenters have taken
their full Share in the Defence of it.
When Mr. *Collins* attempted to undermine the *Grounds and Reafons* of our
Faith, the various Anfwers written by
Diffenters did not difcover any Want of
Zeal for our holy Religion. And when
Chandler the Bifhop wrote his Letter of
Thanks to Chandler the Prefbyter, for
his learned Defence of it, *he* furely
would not have wifhed that his fellow
Labourer in the common Caufe, fhould
have all his Lifetime remained fubject to
Imprifonment for preaching a Sermon,
and enforcing the Duties of that Gofpel,
the Truth of which he had fo ably
maintained.

AFTER this, when our Religion was
again attacked by Mr. *Tyndal* in his
Chriftianity as old as the Creation, the
Diffenters were again as ready to appear
in its Vindication. We willingly ac-
knowlege

knowlege the Merit of all : but may we
not without being chargeable with Prefumption, afk, whofe Anfwers were more
read, or better approved, than thofe of
Mr. *Simon Brown* and of Dr. *Fofter?*

When Mr. *Pope* faid of this latter,

Let humble *Fofter*, if he will, excell
Ten *Metropolitans* in preaching well,

We know how to afcribe One-half of
this to his Hatred of *Englifh* Bifhops,
and to give a great Part of the reft to
the Warmth of his new-made Friend-
fhip. But fhall Proteftant Divines wifh
the Continuance of a Law, by which
this great Defender of Chriftianity was
liable at any Time to be fent to Jail,
whom Papifts themfelves have treated
thus refpectfully !

I MENTION not the impudent Attack
of *Woolfton*, nor the more fubtle one
made by the Author of *Chriftianity not
founded in Argument :* In anfwering
which, *Benfon* and *Lardner* again diftin-
guifhed

guifhed themfelves. But let it not be told in the foreign Languages, into which the Works of Dr. *Lardner* have been tranflated, that the learned Author of the Credibility of the Gofpel Hiftory, was by the Laws of *England* held all his Lifetime fubject to Fines and Imprifonment: and that, though the late Archbifhop, in the moft friendly Correfpondence, frequently acknowleged his Merits, yet his Succeffors all wifh to maintain the Force of a Law, by which he might at any Time have been fent to Newgate.

WHEN the Works of Lord *Bolingbroke*, that great Apoftate from all the Principles of his Education as a Diffenter, a Proteftant, and a Chriftian, were publifhed after his Death; what Divine is there in this Kingdom, who will ftand forth and fay, that the Work of Dr. *Leland* would not have done him Honour? But *Leland*, though a Proteftant Diffenter, was happily removed out of the Reach of Penal Laws, to which others

are

are fubjected. So too was *Duchal* in the latter Part of his Life, and fo was *Abernethy*, whofe Sermons having been preached in *Ireland*, gained him Honour and general Efteem only, without the Danger of Imprifonment.

UNDER an Accufation of fo reproach-ful a Nature as that of Deifm, the Dif-fenters hope, that they may appeal to their Writings, without incurring the Charge of Vanity or Prefumption. They wifh not to compare themfelves with the Numbers of great Men in the Eftablifh-ment: but what is there to be found in the Works of thefe their departed Friends, or what was there in their Conduct, which could afford any the leaft Ground to bring their Chriftianity into Queftion? Some of thefe fpent long laborious Lives in the Defence of our holy Religion *. The reft were employed in preaching the Duties of it to their feveral Hearers; and

---

* Dr. Lardner was Writing to near his Eightieth Year.

all

all of thefe we truft lived and died in
the Faith of *Chrift*, though they would
never fubfcribe their Affent to any thing
but *his Gofpel*.

WHEN we heard well-meaning High
Church Country Gentlemen fet us forth
as wild Enthufiafts, and Fifth-monarchy
Men; when People that died a hundred
Years ago, Anceftors of we know not
whom, were raifed to Light again, to
fit for *our* Pictures, and we were drawn
with all the Attributes of Fanaticifm; we
thought the Painter injudicious in going
fo far out of the way to make his Picture
unlike; but felt no Difpofition to be
offended at the meer Effect of the narrow Prejudices of Education, and a pro-
found Ignorance of every Thing relating to us. But when Men of Read-
ing, who pretend to know fomething of
us, when Divines, who from their Station fhould be Examples of Chriftian
Charity, when thefe have given Indul-
gence to the moft injurious Reflections;
we have then furely a Right to maintain

H   our

our Integrity; and to appeal to the more impartial Judgment of the Public, to determine whether our Writings have been such, as to mark us with the Character of Deifts, or to fet us fo much below the common Standard of Mankind.

BUT whatever may be the Defects of our Minifters, or how far foever they may fall fhort of other great Divines in their Learning or their Preaching, in their Faith or in their Lives, Fines and Imprifonments are not the natural Means to make them wifer. Nor are thefe furely the proper Powers, which Gentlemen and Scholars, valuing themfelves upon a liberal Education, would wifh to retain over fuch as happen to differ from them; or fit Punifhments, to which they can think, that other Gentlemen of a liberal Education ought to be fubjected. Leaft of all are they the *Chriftian* Means of Conviction, or expreffive of that *Spirit of Meeknefs*, which the Gofpel prefcribes, as the Method of inftructing and reclaiming thofe that be in Error.

UPON

Upon the whole, Men fond of Power over others, may weave as many political or theological Cobwebs as they pleafe; but Truth and Right will eafily pafs through them all. Party Rage and a fudden Frenzy of the Times may practife it; but the cool Senfe of Mankind will never warrant, the committing a Chriftian Divine to Jail for preaching a Chriftian Sermon. If no Man's calm Reafon will juftify the Practice, then what can be the Ground of retaining a Law for it? A Law, which originally was a Law of Tyrants; founded only on Revenge, and tending only to Oppreffion? a Law, which being directly contrary to the Spirit of Chriftianity, and originally made ufe of for the Deftruction of Proteftantifm, muft be a Difgrace to the Church inftead of a Support to it, and what every good Churchman therefore ought to wifh to fee removed.

POSTSCRIPT.

A Very miſtaken Repreſentation of the Proceedings of the Diſſenting Miniſters upon this Affair, makes it neceſſary to relate the following Particulars.

IMMEDIATELY after the Debate in the Houſe of Commons upon the Petition of the Clergy of the Church of *England*, ſome of the Diſſenting Miniſters, who heard that Debate, conſulted with others of their Brethren, whether they ought not to take the Benefit of the preſent Diſpoſition of the Houſe, and petition for that Relief, which they had ſo long deſired, and had been waiting for a proper Opportunity to obtain.

IN theſe Conſultations it ſoon occurred, that there was not Time to take the Aſſiſtance of their Brethren in the Country, and make it ſo general a Concern as they wiſhed it to be, before the laſt Day of receiving Petitions would be over.

over. They therefore laid aside the Thought of applying during the present Seffion: but resolved to call a Meeting of the Diffenting Minifters in and about *London*, to take their Opinion on preparing a Petition for the next Seffion: And agreed that, Summons's fhould accordingly be iffued for the following *Thurfday*.

In this Interval, fome others of the *London* Minifters appointed a Meeting for the *Wednefday*. At that Meeting fome new Intelligence was given of the favourable Difpofition of Government; with the Hope that my Lords the Bifhops might not oppofe them, and with the Offer of a Perfon in high Station to bring in their Bill by Way of Motion, which can be done at any Time of the Seffion. This Intelligence was ftated in fuch a Manner, as to leave no Ground of Blame on thofe who gave it, nor any Imputation of Failure of Promife in thofe to whom it related. But it was fuch Intelligence, as prudent Men would juftly Act upon, in a Matter of this Nature.

And

And many of the Ministers thought, that they should be wanting in the Duty, they owed to Themselves, to their Brethren, and to their Successors, if they did not improve the present favourable Conjuncture. It was accordingly put to the Vote: and of Fifty present, all agreed, except one only, to the following Resolutions: *That the taking off the Subscription required of Protestant Dissenting Ministers, and the obtaining Relief for Tutors and Schoolmasters, are very desirable and important Objects: That Application should be made to Parliament for those Purposes: and that a Committee should be chosen to manage the Affair, with Power to summon the general Body as they should see Occasion.* A Committee of Fifteen out of the three Denominations was immediately chosen. And about Twenty other Ministers, who were not present at the *Wednesday's* Meeting, came on *Thursday* to the Chairman, and all signified their Approbation of the Design.

FROM

FROM the Circumſtances of this Tranſ-action, the Reader ſees, that none but the *London* Miniſters could have been concerned in this Application : the Sud-denneſs of the Reſolution affording them no Time to inform their Brethren in the Country of the Motives to that Determi-nation. The Diſſenting Laity are not affected by this Bill, any otherwiſe than as they wiſh well to their Miniſters.

THE whole of this Application, there-fore, reſted originally with the *London* Miniſters, and with them only.

THE Liſt of allowed Miniſters of the three Denominations in and about *Lon-don*, conſiſts of Ninety Five. Seventy of theſe had declared their Opinions, with only one diſſentient Voice. In the ſubſequent Meetings, the greateſt Num-ber of Hands, held up againſt any one Queſtion propoſed, was only Six : nor did any one of theſe at any Meeting declare the leaſt Diſapprobation of the above Vote,

Vote, except the single One before mentioned, who yet attended at them all.

WHATEVER, therefore, may have been
suggested to the contrary; or how hardily
soever some Things may have been af-
ferted, no one Measure has been adopted
by the Body of *London* Ministers, for
these Fifty Years past, which has been
undertaken and profecuted with a more
general Concurrence.

A BILL.

A

B I L L,

INTITULED

An Act for the further Relief of His Majesty's Protestant Subjects, dissenting from the Church of England.

WHEREAS by an Act made in the First Year of the Reign of King *William* and Queen *Mary*, intituled, " An Act for exempt-
" ing Their Majesties Protestant Subjects, dif-
" fenting from the Church of *England*, from the
" Penalties of certain Laws," Persons dissent-
ing from the Church of *England*, in holy Orders, or pretended holy Orders, or pretending to holy Orders, Preachers or Teachers of any Congre-
gations of dissenting Protestants, are required, in Order to be entitled to certain Exemptions, Benefits, Privileges, and Advantages, to declare their Approbation of, and to subscribe the Arti-
cles of Religion mentioned in, the Statute made in the Thirteenth Year of the Reign of Queen *Elizabeth*, except as in the said Act, made in the First Year of the Reign of King *William* and Queen *Mary*, is excepted: **And whereas** many such Persons scruple to declare their Ap-

I   probation

probation of, and to subscribe the said Articles, not excepted as aforesaid; for giving Ease to such scrupulous Persons in the Exercise of Religion,

May it please Your MAJESTY,

That it may be **enacted ; and be it enacted** by the King's Most Excellent Majesty, by and with the Advice and Consent of the Lords Spiritual and Temporal, and Commons, in this present Parliament assembled, and by the Authority of the same, That so much of the said Act made in the First Year of the Reign of King *William* and Queen *Mary*, as relates to the said Articles, or to any of them, shall be, and the same is hereby repealed.

And be it further enacted by the Authority aforesaid, That every Person dissenting from the Church of *England* in holy Orders, or pretended holy Orders, or pretending to holy Orders, and every Preacher or Teacher of any Congregation of dissenting Protestants, who shall take the Oaths, and make and subscribe the Declaration against Popery, required by the said Act made in the First Year of the Reign of King *William* and Queen *Mary*, to be taken, made, and subscribed by Protestant dissenting Ministers, and shall also make and subscribe a Declaration in the Words, or to the Effect, following; *videlicet,*

I A B declare, as in the Presence of Almighty God, that I believe that the Holy Scriptures of the Old and New Testament contain a Revelation of
the

the Mind and Will of God, and that I receive them as the Rule of my Faith and Practice.

Shall be, and such Person is hereby declared to be, intitled to all the Exemptions, Benefits, Privileges, and Advantages, granted to Protestant dissenting Ministers by the said Act, made in the First Year of the Reign of King *William* and Queen *Mary*; and by an Act made in the Tenth Year of the Reign of Queen *Anne*, intituled, ' An Act for preserving the Protestant ' Religion, by better securing the Church of ' *England* as by Law established, and for con- ' firming the Toleration granted to Protestant ' Dissenters, by an Act, intituled, " An Act for " exempting Their Majesties Protestant Sub- " jects, dissenting from the Church of *England*, " from the Penalties of certain Laws, and for " supplying the Defects thereof; and for the " further securing the Protestant Succession, by " requiring the Practisers of the Law in *North* " *Britain* to take the Oaths, and subscribe the " Declaration therein mentioned;" and the Justices of the Peace, at the General Sessions of the Peace to be holden for the County or Place where any Protestant dissenting Minister shall live, are hereby required to tender and admi- nister the said last-mentioned Declaration to such Minister, upon his offering himself to make and subscribe the same, and thereof to keep a Re- gister; and such Minister shall not give or pay as a Fee or Reward, to any Officer or Officers belonging to the Court aforesaid, above the Sum of Sixpence for his or their Entry of such Minister's making and subscribing the said last-

men-

mentioned Declaration, and taking the Oaths, and making and subscribing the Declaration against Popery, required by the said Act made in the First Year of the Reign of King *William* and Queen *Mary*, to be taken, made, and subscribed by Protestant dissenting Ministers, nor above the Sum of Sixpence for any Certificate thereof, to be made out and signed by the Officer or Officers of the said Court.

And whereas by an Act made in the Thirteenth and Fourteenth Years of King *Charles* the Second, intituled, " An Act for the Uniformity of Public Prayers, and Administration of " Sacraments, and other Rites and Ceremonies ; " and for establishing the Form of making, or- " daining, and consecrating Bishops, Priests, and " Deacons, in the Church of *England*," **it is enacted**, That if any Person who is by that Act disabled to preach any Lecture or Sermon, shall, during the Time that he shall continue and remain so disabled, preach any Sermon or Lecture, that then, for every such Offence, the Person and Persons so offending shall suffer Three Months Imprisonment in the County Gaol, without Bail or Mainprize : And by an Act made in the Fifteenth Year of the same Reign, intituled, " An Act for Relief of such " Persons as, by Sickness or other Impediment, " were disabled from subscribing the Declaration " in the Act of Uniformity, and Explanation " of Part of the said Act," it is declared and enacted, That the Penalties by the said Act made in the Thirteenth and Fourteenth Years of the Reign of King *Charles* the Second, to be inflicted upon

any

any Perfon difabled by the faid laft-mentioned
Act to preach, for any Offence againft the faid
laft-mentioned Act, fhall, in like Manner, be
inflicted upon every Perfon fo offending, that is
prohibited by the faid laft-mentioned Act to
preach.

𝕬𝖓𝖉 𝖜𝖍𝖊𝖗𝖊𝖆𝖘 no exprefs Provifion is made
in and by the faid Act made in the Firft Year of
the Reign of King *William* and Queen *Mary*,
for exempting any Proteftant diffenting Minifters
from fuch Imprifonment ; 𝖇𝖊 𝖎𝖙 𝖊𝖓𝖆𝖈𝖙𝖊𝖉 by
the Authority aforefaid, That no Proteftant
diffenting Minifter, who fhall qualify himfelf
as aforefaid, fhall be liable to be imprifoned by
virtue of the aforefaid Acts made in the Reign of
King *Charles* the Second, or of either of them,
for preaching any Sermon or Lecture in any
Congregation of Proteftant Diffenters : And for
preventing Perfons from fraudulently qualifying
themfelves as Diffenting Minifters, 𝖇𝖊 𝖎𝖙 𝖋𝖚𝖗𝖙𝖍𝖊𝖗
𝖊𝖓𝖆𝖈𝖙𝖊𝖉 by the Authority aforefaid, That every
Perfon who fhall offer to qualify himfelf as a
diffenting Minifter at the General Seffion of
the Peace, fhall, if thereunto required, pro-
duce to the Juftices of the Peace, at the faid
Seffion affembled, a Teftimonial, figned by
Three or more Proteftant diffenting Minifters,
and fpecifying the refpective Places where they
ftatedly officiate, in the Words, or to the Effect
following, *videlicet*;

WE, whofe Names are under written, being
Proteftant diffenting Minifters, hereby certify, That
we know A B, and that to the beft of our Know-
ledge, he is a Perfon of a good moral and chriftian
Charac-

Character, and that we receive and acknowledge him as a Protestant dissenting Minister.

Witnefs our Hands this   Day of

And be it further enacted by the Authority aforefaid, That no diffenting Minifter, who fhall qualify himfelf· as aforefaid, nor any other Proteftant, diffenting from the Church of *England*, who, befides taking the Oaths mentioned in the faid Act made in the firft Year of the Reign of King *William* and Queen *Mary*, and making and fubfcribing the Declaration mentioned in the Statute made in the Thirtieth Year of the Reign of King *Charles* the Second, intituled, " An Act for the more effectual preferv- " ing the King's Perfon and Government, by " difabling Papifts from fitting in either Houfe " of Parliament," fhall make and fubfcribe the Declaration above fet forth, fhall be profecuted in any Court whatfoever, for teaching and inftructing Youth as a Tutor or Schoolmafter ; but every fuch Minifter and fuch other Perfon fhall have full Liberty to teach and inftruct ·Youth as a Tutor or Schoolmafter ; any Law or Statute to the Contrary thereof notwith- ftanding: And the Juftices of the Peace, at the General Seffion of the Peace to be holden for the County or Place where any Proteftant, who not being a diffenting Minifter, fhall be defirous of making and fubfcribing the faid laft-mentioned Declaration, fhall live, are hereby required to tender and adminifter the faid laft-mentioned Declaration to fuch Proteftant, upon his offering himfelf to make and fubfcribe the fame, and thereof to keep a Regifter ; and fuch Proteftant fhall not give or pay, as a Fee or Reward

to

to any Officer or Officers belonging to the fame Court, above the Sum of Sixpence for his or their Entry of fuch Proteftants making and fub-fcribing the faid laft-mentioned Declaration, and taking the Oaths, and making and fubfcribing the Declaration againft Popery, required by the faid Act made in the Firft Year of the Reign of King *William* and Queen *Mary*, to be taken, made, and fubfcribed by Proteftant Diffenters ; nor above the further Sum of Sixpence for any Certificate thereof, to be made out and figned by the Officer or Officers of the faid Court.

Provided always, That nothing in this Act fhall extend, or be conftrued to extend, to the enabling any Perfon diffenting from the Church of *England* to obtain or hold the Maf-terfhip of any College or School of Royal Foun-dation, or of any other endowed College or School for the Education of Youth, other than fuch as have been or hereafter may be inftituted by, or intended for, the immediate Ufe and Benefit of Proteftant Diffenters.

And whereas it hath been doubted, whether the faid Act made in the Firft Year of the Reign of King *William* and Queen *Mary* be a Publick or a Private Act; *be it declared and en-acted* by the Authority aforefaid, That the faid Act, and alfo this prefent Act, fhall be adjudged, deemed, and taken to be Publick Acts, and fhall be judicially taken Notice of as fuch by all Judges, Juftices, and other Perfons whom-foever, without fpecially pleading them, or either of them.

F I N I S.